Bob & the Final Reveal

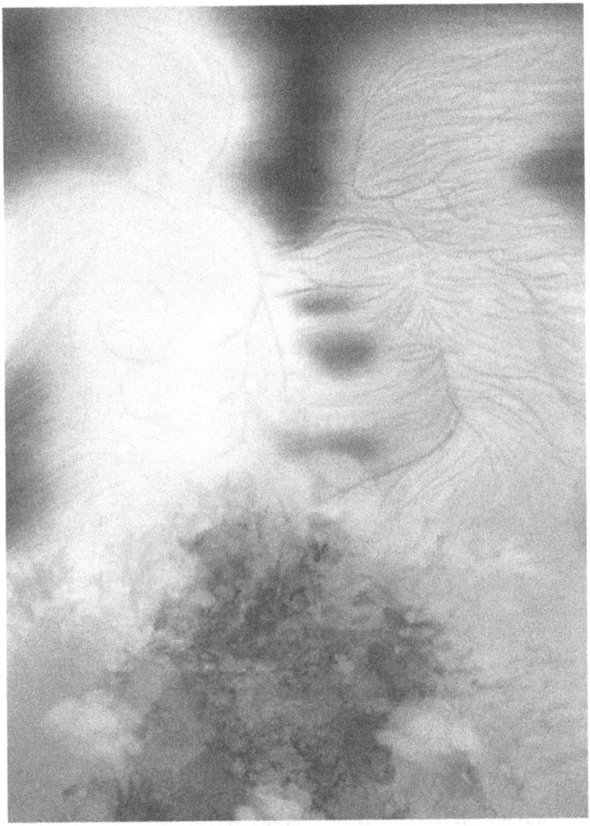

Author: Shayne T Pattie

Editors: Charmaine Hawthorn & Peta-Jane Pattie

Cover Illustrator: Angela Pattie

Preface

Is energy ascension the final evolutionary step for humankind? Throughout history, civilisations have pondered the nature of existence. Are we merely biological machines, complex biochemical networks, or something far beyond. Science, philosophy, and spirituality have all sought to define consciousness, yet no definitive answers exist.

If thought, memory, and emotion are nothing more than patterns of electrical impulses, then is it possible for a sentient being to transcend its physical form and exist purely as energy, while still retaining self-awareness, identity, and individuality?

Modern science has already explored the various mechanisms of energy transfer within the human body. Every heartbeat, every thought, and every breath are all powered by biochemical reactions. From ATP synthesis in mitochondria to neural synapses firing in the brain, we are already, in many ways, beings of energy. But could evolution take this further?

Could the next step in human transformation be a transition beyond flesh and matter, beyond death itself, perhaps towards a form that exists entirely within the fabric of energy?

If such an ascension were possible, what would this mean for our understanding of life and death? Would mortality cease to exist, or would it take on a new meaning altogether? Could an entity of pure energy still experience the range of emotions that many animals including humans can experience such as love, loss, or longing? Or would these emotions dissolve, revealing a new form of consciousness unimproved or unhampered by emotions?

Furthermore, if the essence of our reality is nothing more than energy vibrating at different frequencies, then are we already existing in a spectrum beyond our comprehension? What if the boundaries between life and death, creation and destruction, are simply thresholds of energy transformation?

A physics theory postulates that energy cannot be created or destroyed, only changed. In the cycle of existence, does destruction ever lead to rebirth, or is it merely a necessary phase in an endless process of change?

This exploration challenges not only what we understand about evolution, but what it means to be 'alive'. If the journey of consciousness is an ever-expanding force, then perhaps ascension is not an end, but a doorway into an unimaginable new frontier.

Finally, is 'Multiversal Theory' a stretch or a theory of energy? If a multiverse can exist, can the same being exist across universes, and if so, can they influence their other selves?

Table of Contents

Bob Flees

Bob had returned to Earth from Sodatsu in the hope of writing some of his previous wrongs. He had hoped that by doing this he could then refocus on a new goal. However, when he accidently triggered a massive change in the person known as Clarence (which then led to Clarence dying), Bob was filled with hope that he might be able to bring Jay back to life.

This oxymoronic thought was triggered by memories of Neo-Ronin's initial conversation with Bob about energy manipulation, and Neo-Ronin's last conversation with Bob about side effects of lower lifeforms touching Bob's new energy form.

This new hope gave Bob a new purpose. However, when Bob decides it is time to leave Earth to return to Sodatsu, he hears a voice sounding full of hatred as if from out of nowhere but quite nearby.

The voice then says, "I am not finished with you yet Bob".

Bob was startled. He turned around to see an odd being in front of him. The being itself wasn't exactly like Bob but was also no longer human. Bob could see that where the human Clarence once stood, there now appeared to be a form of energy being, both similar and very different to Bob. Bob barely understood his own energy form and its powers. He felt that there was almost no chance of him understanding Clarence's new form.

Clarence appeared to be a translucent red colour, still for now at least, only vaguely resembling a human in shape. If Bob was not currently an energy being, who had previously been abducted by aliens and who just saw a human change colour multiple times before dying, he would have assumed that this was someone using fancy lighting to trick him.

However, Bob began to feel like his own entire energy form was being slowly sucked towards Clarence like a vacuum cleaner on the lowest possible setting. Bob had no idea what was happening, but he did not like the feeling of it. He only knew one course of action. He knew he had to escape.

Bob felt something that he hadn't felt since he had killed prince Neon. He felt a feeling of fear and powerlessness. Bob decides to listen to what he feels, and he then makes the smart decision to flee. However, before Bob can flee, Clarence screams at Bob "What Am I"? Bob tries to answer with a calm voice, but it is evident he is not at all calm.

Bob replies "I have no idea. I am sorry for anything I did in the past that seems to have invoked your hatred towards me. I am sorry for what I may have just done to you. However, I am not able to help you. You will need to figure this out on your own, just as I myself am trying to do. I do know that if you find a way to focus yourself and ground yourself, you might be able to start a new life somewhere, but I am not the person to guide you or to help you. I am sorry".

Utilising his energy form, Bob is eventually able to exit out of the ceiling and towards space as fast as he had ever travelled. As Bob leaves the room, he can still hear Clarence screaming his name, "BOB!!!".

Bob believes that Clarence will not be able to follow him to Sodatsu but also wants to ensure the safety of Sodatsu just in case. Bob is still feeling a little scared from what has just occurred and is still somewhat confused. However, Bob tries to focus on escaping Clarence, ensuring he is not being followed by

Clarence, with the goal of returning to Sodatsu being his priority.

Bob then travels to the sun at the centre of the solar system, thinking that the sun might destroy Clarence should he choose to follow Bob. When Bob arrives near the sun he turns and sees nothing following him, giving him a brief sense of relief. Bob then rests for what feels like several moments for him, however, since time doesn't affect him, this could have been days or weeks. Whilst resting near the sun, Bob feels a minor energy burst in his body but ignores this.

Bob continues travelling from solar system to solar system towards the centre of the Milky Way galaxy. Bob stops near each solar system's sun to ensure he is not being followed.

Bob no longer sees suns as he did as a human. As an energy being, he now sees things as energy frequencies, and when he saw Clarence, he saw an odd combination of what looked and felt like an absence of energy, yet Bob was still able to understand that Clarence's new form was a red translucent colour. The combination of emotions, the context, his own thoughts and this confusing development, fuelled his sense of fear and powerlessness regarding Clarence and the potential danger he represented. Bob felt that if Clarence was as powerful as himself, then he and many others would be in danger. For now, however, he had to focus on reaching Sodatsu as his main goal.

Because of his way of seeing his reality, Bob pays almost no attention to what the differing suns look like. Even when he had previously wondered throughout space, his mind was often filled with thoughts of himself or others, and rarely did Bob just enjoys the sights through his different vision.

Almost every time Bob stops near a sun on his way back to Sodatsu, he notices a minor energy burst in his body, and each time he ignores this, with his thoughts again preoccupied, but this time preoccupied on being followed by a new possibly more powerful being. Albeit a being that he had accidently created. One that arose because Bob didn't pay attention and ignored king Neo-Ronin's warning.

Bob finally reaches the centre of the Milky Way galaxy and sees that nothing is following him. He then goes through the black hole on his way to Sodatsu. Bob has now travelled from Sodatsu to Earth passing through various black holes and passing near many suns. He has also now travelled at a slower rate back towards Sodatsu stopping by many suns and then travelling through multiple black holes.

After travelling several galaxies and entering several black holes, Bob notices a slight change in himself. He feels smaller and denser. He had been busy before with his own thoughts both on his travels to Earth and with his travels from Earth and hadn't taken any notice of his internal changes. He had previously believed that his new energy form was the highest step in evolution. He felt that his new form was incapable of change or adaptation. However, now those changes had become more evident for Bob. He felt that he had begun to evolve further.

Bob had barely begun to understand his own energy being self before, but these new changes made Bob feel that he was becoming more, again. Bob feels that he needs to investigate this further. He felt like he had shrunk but simultaneously now had more mass. He felt that his powers and entire being had now increased not only in power but also in potential. He is curious as to what a pure energy lifeform such as himself could possibly evolve into. After all, what was more advantageous than pure energy?

Bob also wants to visit Jay and Sodatsu. Bob still misses Jay and the potential life Sodatsu's prince had taken from him. Bob's need to see if he can bring Jay back to life outweighs his curiosity about his new potential evolution or ascension. So, Bob decides to put the energy questions aside for now and he travels to Sodatsu. Again, Bob only stops on occasion as a precaution to ensure he wasn't being followed by Clarence.

Despite all his power, Bob was still somehow driven by emotion. The logical option would have been to master his denser form. The logical option for Bob would have been to understand himself better in the hope he could utilise this new power to improve the chances of bringing Jay back to life. However, because of Bob's longing for Jay, his decision making had been based on his emotional need.

Bob did not want anyone on Sodatsu to know about Clarence and he also did not want anyone to be harmed by Clarence. He still felt guilty about Jay dying, as he felt that if he hadn't pursued a romantic relationship with her, then Sodatsu's prince would not have targeted her, and she could still be contributing her scientific expertise for the betterment of their planet. He did not want to be responsible for more Sodatsu beings' deaths.

Bob also felt guilt for what had happened both with and to Clarence. As he is barely able to understand why Clarence seemed to hate him so much. Bob had theorised it had something to do with Jessie, but was unsure how Clarence would have found out or deduced Bob's influence regarding the circumstances of Jessie's death.

Bob also felt that Clarence had been unlucky. Bob felt that if he had of listened to king Neo-Ronin's warning about touching lower lifeforms as an energy being, then Clarence would still be alive as a human and Bob would have nothing to worry about.

Bob did not think about the potential deaths elsewhere that Clarence might cause. Bob did not think about Earth much anymore. Bob had now been able to say goodbye to his parents, and he was glad he did, despite their difficult relationship. Bob had been able to say goodbye to Jessie at their grave and even share everything that had happened up until that point. However, now Sodatsu had become his new home, and Earth was just a memory.

Bob has one thought in mind, restarting a life on Sodatsu, hopefully with Jay. Bob did not think about the practical barriers to having a relationship with Jay, even if he was able to bring her back to life. He did not think practically at all. He had channelled his grief and loss and placed it all into an unknown type of hope. The type of hope that is unachievable and potentially dangerous. The type of hope that will impact him in the near future. The type of hope that will inadvertently hurt more lifeforms across universes, but potentially help a stranger in the distant, distant future, in a universe far away.

Bob Visits Jay

After his long travel with many and varied stops, Bob finally reaches Sodatsu and floats around for a small while. He then decides it would be best for him to speak with the king and with Zion, so he doesn't scare the population. He also feels he should speak with Zion before he visits where Jay is now located because he feels responsible for Jay's death. Also, he is unsure exactly where Jay is buried and wants to find this out before he floats around the planet aimlessly.

Bob floats to Zion's laboratory. He notices Zion hard at work and interrupts him anyway. Zion looks up and is shocked to see Bob. Zion previously didn't get a chance to have a full conversation with Bob after Jay's death and was hoping to speak with the Bob again in the future. Zion and Bob then discuss what had been happening since Bob's departure.

Bob discusses how he travelled back to his home planet after wandering around space for a while, how he said goodbye to his parents, how he visited a deceased friend's grave on Earth and how he attempted to apologise to a friend's previous manager. Bob decides it best not to share the events that followed, involving Clarence. Bob also shares that he felt he had to return to Sodatsu as Earth no longer felt like home.

Zion enquires about Bob's travels from a scientific perspective. Zion asks Bob about how gravity and other forms of energy impact Bob's new energy form. Bob discusses that initially he hadn't noticed any changes but on his return journey from Earth to Sodatsu, he had begun noticing slight changes in his density and power. Bob explains how he feels simultaneously heavier and smaller, to which Zion confirms the latter. Bob also reiterates how he now feels more powerful than before and feels he may be evolving or ascending again. Despite Zion being curious as to the causes and implications of this he instead chooses not to explore this further without the king's approval. Instead, Zion decides to speak with Bob about the changes on Sodatsu.

Zion is glad to see Bob has returned. He shares how there had been many changes in Sodatsu since the war where Bob saved most of the planet. Zion discusses how he had recently been working with several very promising young Sodatsu beings living the old ways, and how these in many ways reminded Zion of Bob because of their good work ethic and their eagerness to improve and learn. Bob and Zion both then reminisce about Bob's time on

Sodatsu as a human and about Zion's reluctance and eventual leadership.

Zion then goes quiet. After several moments Zion asks Bob some questions about Jay. Zion asks if Bob and Jay were up to anything other than study, and if so, what other activities he needed to know about. Zion then shares that he wants the truth even if it is difficult to hear. Bob then pauses and after several moments decides to tell Zion almost everything. He asks Zion to sit down and then begins to answer Zion's question.

Initially, Bob is hesitant. He is unsure how to explain the relationship between Jay and himself, to Zion. Eventually, with verbal prodding from Zion, Bob begins. Bob explains that Jay and Bob had initially become close and that it was Bob that pursued Jay romantically. Bob explains that initially Jay was open to this from an academic and scientific perspective, but eventually Jay shared romantic feelings for Bob. Bob shares how Jay and Bob continued their relationship in secret as they both knew it wouldn't be accepted. They had been seeing each other for a very long time prior to the war.

Bob shares how he and Jay finally decided to share with Zion that Jay was pregnant from the natural ways of reproduction and that on the day they were supposed to tell everything to Zion, the civil war broke out. Bob shares that Jay was nervous but excited to inform Zion about the pregnancy but had waited as long as she did because of the perceived biases and conflict with the then Sodatsu cultural practices. This combined with Bob being a lower lifeform at the time, Jay also felt a level of embarrassment despite her intense feelings for Bob.

Bob shares that he regrets he couldn't protect Jay from prince Neon. Bob then shares how great an influence Jay had been. He discusses how Jay had helped him to become a better person. Bob explains that it was Jay's influence that led him to attempting to make peace with the prince without further bloodshed, and that it was Jay that helped Bob find peace within himself before the war.

Zion shares that he had some suspicions similar to that of what he was being told, but did not realise the full extent. He feels somewhat betrayed by Bob for taking advantage of Zion's kindness as it was Zion who had let Bob enter his residence and meet his family. Zion has a mixture of foreign and uncomfortable emotions surging through his body. Zion blames himself and Bob for Jay's death but keeps this thought to himself.

Zion then shares with Bob that he now has intense emotions towards Bob that he does not feel comfortable with. Zion then thanks Bob for his honesty and asks Bob to give him some space for a while. Bob accepts this and floats away.

Bob then floats to the king's residence and gets the king's attention. The king is surprised and almost excited to speak with Bob. Bob then shares his adventures of travelling to Earth and back again sharing the same story he had initially told Zion. Bob once again leaves out the Clarence situation. Bob also chooses not to discuss anything regarding Jay and their relationship in case it negatively affects the king's opinion of him and leads to his exile from the planet.

The king is excited to share all that had transpired since Bob left. The king and his guards take Bob on a tour around most of the planet showing how the old ways and new ways had begun working together. The king shares how Bob's conversation after his ascension and the events of the civil war led the king to seek balance from a wider lens.

The easiest example of change that the king shows Bob is the rezoning along the previous unofficial border. This rezoning reduced the inequality regarding fertile soil, leading to some improvements in the quality of life for both the old and new ways and also opened up both social and technological improvements.

The king shares that technology and resource efficiency initially became delayed during the restructuring of the schools and rezoning of areas along the previous boarder, but recently there had been several breakthroughs because of these changes. Some of these breakthroughs led to a better understanding of Sodatsu biology regarding the origins and mechanisms of the energy powers and this led to further improvements in life expectancy.

The king also discusses how the Sodatsu plant reproduction is now a choice, with some inhabitants from both the old and new ways asking to have their genome spliced to start a family, and some wanting to practice traditional ways of reproduction.

This has unofficially led to third type of Sodatsu being that appear to be more emotional and harder working than those produced and raised exclusively in the new ways, but also more technologically savvy than those raised exclusively in the old ways. The king feels that perhaps in the near future someone from this "third type" might lead Sodatsu to an even better future.

Several elders of the old ways have also begun visiting the new areas to discuss the history of Sodatsu from their perspective which has led to even further improvements socially between the two dominant cultural practices. The king is curious whether this new way of life might be the answer for balance, and whether this new balance will last.

Bob is amazed at how many changes the king has made since the civil war and how quickly these changes seemed to have helped. Bob also reminds the king of the pitfalls of seeking balance too much and how the act of seeking the perfect balance might have been a contributing factor of the previous civil war. The king allows himself to laugh and acknowledges this.

The king comments that Bob appears smaller since he last left Sodatsu. Bob confirms this and shares how he also feels denser and somehow more powerful, although he is having difficulty explaining why. Neo-Ronin suggests that if Bob has time, he should visit Zion to explore Bob's energy changes, as this might be helpful for Bob, but also helpful for Sodatsu's technology. The king then reminds Bob to be careful while on Sodatsu and to not touch other living beings on Sodatsu when he leaves. Eventually the king says goodbye to Bob and returns to his quarters. Bob then floats away to his goal location.

Bob floats to where he was told Jay had been buried by Zion. During daylight Bob talks to Jay's grave about what had transpired since he left Sodatsu. Bob shares his travels, his decision to return to Earth, and his accidental creation, in Clarence. Bob explains that he is also changing, and how no one yet understands why, and how he hopes that Zion might be able to help in the future. Bob also shares his real reason for returning to Sodatsu and hopes that if it works Jay will be understanding.

Unknown to Bob and most lifeforms in this universe an immense being had been slowly travelling between universes and was now in Bob's. This being's very existence increased the emotions of all that lived in the universe it was visiting, allowing for emotions to drive the lifeforms behaviours.

Bob then waits until it is as dark as possible and fortunately for Bob, it is the darkest he has ever seen Sodatsu, almost ominously so. Since Bob does not hold any spiritual beliefs, he ignores the ominous feeling and then attempts to bring Jay back to life using his new energy form. Bob uses his energy form and allows his body to slowly phase through the ground towards Jay. When he sees Jay's body, he notices an absence of energy. He notices that the only energy around Jay seems to be coming from the ground and not from Jay herself.

Bob is now much less confident about his ability to bring Jay back to life as he no longer sees any energy within Jay's decaying body to work with. Unperturbed he touches Jay's body hoping that his energy will transfer into her and fix her current state.

Unfortunately, for everyone, Bob discovers the hard way, that his new energy lifeform is only capable of manipulating the energy in things that are alive to help them grow, change size, be cured of disease or die. When a being is dead, Bob is only able to manipulate the energy in the dead things which only speeds up the process of decay. This saddens Bob. Bob also discovers that when a being has no energy left, attempting to feed it energy only creates a rebound effect. Ignoring the initial rebound, Bob tries again and again.

Eventually he has become careless about how much energy he transfers towards Jay's decaying body. In an act of desperation, Bob accidentally causes a loud explosion from the unexpected energy burst and subsequent rebound.

Instead of bringing Jay back to life, Bob accidently destroys what remained of Jay and the unborn child in the grave. This causes Bob immense sadness, although he is unable to express this outwardly. The surrounding area is scorched from the accidental energy blast and all other graves nearby have now been destroyed. A scorched crater now lay where Jay's and all the other graves previously were.

A lot of the Sodatsu beings hear the explosion. The king's guards think this to be a potential attack and rally their numbers. Zion is the first to arrive at the site of the noise. Upon seeing Bob and the crater now surrounding him, Zion is beyond angry.

He had tried to be understanding when he found out about Jay and Bob. He had kept a calm exterior and tried to be understanding about the situation despite his internal negative feelings towards Bob.

However, now he lets his frustrations known and blames Bob for the prince targeting Jay. Zion screams at Bob from a distance letting everyone around them know that Zion blames Bob for everything that happened to Jay. Zion then pulls out a new untested weapon and fires an energy blade towards Bob.

However, in Bob's new form, especially with the increased density, the energy blades hit Bob and seems to disintegrate on impact. This only angers Zion more leading to him increasing his screaming. Zion's screaming draws several of the king's guards, and Zion then calls for the king to deal with Bob.

Clarence's Chemical Energy Being

Following the interactions with Bob's energy being and the unexpected ascension, Clarence had become a form of chemical energy being. Clarence is now almost entirely fuelled by emotions and is now a being capable of the destruction of energy at the deepest and smallest level. His chemical energy form appears to be held together like the eye of a hurricane or cyclone, where it is relatively stable in the centre whilst simultaneously destroying everything around it. Clarence's chemical energy form appears to break many of the rules of physics currently understood by both humans and Sodatsu beings. It is this very destruction that holds Clarence together and strengthens him.

Initially, Clarence wanted to follow after Bob and destroy him, but after Bob disappears, Clarence decides he will practice mastering his new form so he will become strong enough to destroy Bob once and for all. Also, Clarence doesn't know how to move in his new form.

Clarence spends many days learning to control his new movement. Initially, whenever Clarence attempts to move in any direction he falls through the floor and the earth. On several occasions while he was phasing, he phased into the ocean accidently destroying a small area of ocean and life around him.

However, as Clarence was still learning about his powers, he did not notice the destruction that is left behind. His phasing and accidental destruction was also enough to impact several tectonic plates. Again, unknown to Clarence this tiny destruction and interference of the tectonic plates, accidently led to several previously dormant volcanos spewing lava and gas in their wake. His travels through the Earth, also led to minor damage through all the layers of the Earth including atmosphere, and the Earth's core. This led to lots of damage weeks later from tsunamis in Japan increasing in intensity, to ocean temperatures rising dramatically.

However, fortunately for Clarence his falling always finished with him returning roughly to his original starting location, his bedroom. Clarence has difficulty focusing but eventually, he notices that thinking of Bob and the anger Bob triggers internally helps him to focus. After spending the rest of the night focusing on movement, he is able to move in his direction of choice.

Once Clarence has mastered basic movement, he recalls himself falling through the earth and buildings. He eventually understands that he is now able to phase through any material similar to how Bob had disappeared, but only when he is able to focus on the direction that he is travelling so that he doesn't fall through the earth again.

Next Clarence notices that there is now a tiny, almost invisible red residue from where he had phased, and he notices it on the floor and the ceiling. It appears almost to be a burn mark, but Clarence is unsure what exactly it is, but he does understand that he caused it by his phasing. Clarence still holds most of his humanity and the values that went along with this.

Worried about potential damage to property and other people, Clarence decides to travel to a remote location. Clarence remembers that Bob's car was found on the town's hill (on the far side that almost no one travelled to or explored) and decides that this would be the closest and safest location to continue his self-directed training.

Clarence travels to the furthest side of the town's hill as quick as he can and upon arriving, finds himself somehow able to relax.

The energy he had been keeping in, seems to be released by accident and vaporises much of the surrounding vegetation. Clarence is thankful no people were around to be injured. Clarence is also shocked at what he had just witnessed. He attempts to vaporise more vegetation but is unable to. He then thinks of Bob which then fills him with anger. Clarence then attempts to relax, and this leads to more vegetation being vaporised.

Clarence is still learning about his powers and doesn't understand that when the object becomes vaporised by him, its energy at the atomic level is destroyed and the object itself turns into nothingness; less visible than dust, it just disappears to the naked eye. He also doesn't yet understand that the more he destroys the greater his power becomes.

Clarence then sees some bits of metal that were never removed from what Clarence assumes to be Bob's destroyed car. He notices that all the vegetation had just been vaporised, but the metal seems to be only singed or rusted, but he is unsure which. Clarence repeats the process of thinking about Bob, filling himself with anger, then attempting to relax. After the third attempt of this process, whilst looking at the metal, he is able to vaporise the metal pieces.

Clarence continues practicing this process until everything within a one-kilometre radius has been vaporised. After what feels like only moments for Clarence, but what has actually been several more days of conscious practice, his powers have increased immensely. He notices that he has now been able destroy a small chunk of the hill in such a way that it now appears to be in the shape of a cave.

Clarence was never a science major, but he had been alive for long enough and been a police officer long enough to have developed superior deductive reasoning. Clarence can understand that he is now capable of vaporising any material, regardless of density. He still has no idea how he exists, what keeps him alive, nor does he have any understanding regarding how he can vaporise any material.

His vision has also changed. Initially, he was able to see the world, mostly as he had as a human. However, as his power grew his vision slowly became distorted and warped. After the most recent vaporisation, his vision has changed completely. Instead of seeing things as they appear to other humans or animals,

Clarence now sees things as energy levels. Whether natural or constructed, the higher energy objects such as electrical wires and suns appear as intense vibrant structures that emit their own light. The greater the level of energy being emitted by the object the brighter the green light it emits. Lower energy objects such as thin blades of grass or single clay bricks, emit a barely visible greyish light. It takes Clarence some time to understand how his new vision works, but eventually his new vision gives him a sense of superiority instead of judgement. He feels he is becoming more, he feels he is becoming closer to that of a god.

He has now started seeing the effects of his vaporisation, but only when he is paying full attention. When he is fully focused, he can now see the green light emitted from materials and lifeforms. As the materials and lifeforms lose their energy, Clarence can see the green light being emitted slowly disappear and slowly become greyish before disappearing completely.

As Clarence is now capable of destroying energy, the green energy being emitted becomes a focus beacon; almost like a moth being attracted to a light or flame, Clarence is becoming attracted to energy, emitted as green light. The more intense and brighter the green light becomes, the more Clarence has an urge to destroy it.

Despite not understanding most of these changes, his new powers fill him with courage which further encourages him to keep up his training. Clarence feels that if he keeps training and improving his mastery over his new form and new powers, he will eventually be strong enough to destroy Bob for good.

The concept of time is no longer relevant to Clarence. He spends several weeks training himself with the goal of improving his destructive powers and abilities. He notices that he is now vaporising objects within a fifty-metre radius without any conscious attempt. It also appears that Clarence has now developed an aura of vaporising destruction that surrounds him.

He likens himself to a cyclone with him being the epicentre and his vaporising aura being the outer coating on the outside. This also encourages Clarence to continue his training but avoid people. Clarence's values regarding human life (except for Bob) are still present, although these values that give importance to human life are slowly fading as his power grows.

Clarence practices floating different distances to understand the range of his vaporisation. It takes several more days, but he notices that the more he thinks of Bob, the further he can vaporise by just existing. He no longer needs to focus the anger and then release it; it is now becoming part of his existence.

He also notices that when he becomes too relaxed by thinking of his past and his favourite police officer related events, or positive memories, he becomes weakened and feels like his energy form is disintegrating. He will not let this happen, he will ensure he does not think of too many good things about his life as a human including memories about the town he grew up in, at least not until Bob is destroyed once and for all.

Clarence eventually understands that to remain alive in whatever state this new living is, he needs to continue fuelling his anger. The easiest tool for Clarence to fuel his anger is thinking of Bob and all the reasons why he hates Bob. Thinking of Bob seems to not only power Clarence's form but also stabilise his form. Clarence is somewhat concerned that if he is successful in killing Bob that he will run out of anger, not realising that he is also powered by the destruction of energy. Clarence does not understand what will happen to his own existence if he ever kills Bob but feels that is a problem for his future self.

It is now silent where Clarence is. Clarence was so busy training that he didn't take notice of time or of any changes that were occurring around him. Clarence didn't see the large number of birds, insects and other animals that he had vaporised during the course of his training. The wild animals that previously roamed the hill, the birds that previously flew overhead, the birds that previously nested in the trees, the trees themselves, the insects that helped to improve the soil and the nutrients in the soil itself, are all vaporised with their energy destroyed.

Several weeks have passed, and Clarence's vaporising aura has increased in power, the land around Clarence begins to become unstable as all material has been vaporised and turned into nothingness; with their atoms destroyed.

Clarence does not want to destroy his town, and without thinking he decides to travel into space as it is the furthest, he can think of to get away from his hometown. Clarence was not sure if he would be able to exist but felt as he no longer needed to breath, eat or go to the toilet, that he should be fine. Without thinking, Clarence travels towards Venus.

Clarence was trying to do the safe and right thing by his town, but as he wasn't focusing on anything except travelling to Venus, Clarence did not notice that his small aura destroyed everything in its path, leading to a small hole in the Earth's atmosphere. Clarence's travels seemed to leave an inverse streak, a clean streak with anything in a certain diameter vaporised into nothing.

This impacted his hometown and Earth as a whole, but many scientists attributed these changes to climate change and nothing more. The number and intensity of storms and fires increased, but governments thought nothing of it, also attributing these to climate change. Several minor satellites were also destroyed, but again this was attributed to malfunctions and even accusations of other nations' interference. Noone had reason to suspect Clarence.

Something about Venus and its unstable and gaseous state appeals to Clarence. Perhaps he feels that Venus is a representation of himself, perhaps it is the closest planet to Earth to travel to, or perhaps the amount of energy being emitted from the gas storms on Venus has attracted Clarence. The sun emits a more intense and brighter green then Venus, but Clarence still has part of his humanity left in him and doesn't want to accidently destroy the sun as he feels it would destroy his hometown.

So, he instead continues his path directly to Venus not taking note of the destruction in front of or behind him and not taking the time to appreciate how amazing it was that he was now able to travel through space, unaided by technology.

To an outsider timing Clarence, it took him approximately three Earth hours, to travel from Lackyer Vale to Venus. Once near Venus, Clarence travels towards it's centre feeling that the planet would allow for immense training and improvement in the control of his powers. Clarence thought that he might struggle with the gas, the variation in gravity, the chemicals or the heat, but he has no difficulty floating in place on Venus.

The opposite seemed to be happening to Clarence. Instead of struggling, the gaseous environment of Venus filled with the ever-changing energy and energy reactions, strengthened Clarence. Again, Clarence has no understanding as to why or how, but he is becoming stronger and not just because of his conscious effort.

Clarence continues training until he is able to disintegrate many of Venus' storms, with thought alone. The green light emitted from Venus' storms slowly turn to greyish light then nothing. Slowly, Venus is becoming quiet.

After even more training on Venus, the planet seems to become silent. The atmosphere on Venus has disintegrated. Where there previously had stood a gaseous unstable planet, there now stood nothing. It took Clarence a small while to realise he was now floating in space with no evidence that a planet ever existed there. Allowing himself to feel perhaps a tiny amount of human emotions other than anger, he is triggered to return home one last time, perhaps to say goodbye to his town and to Earth.

Again, Clarence is unaware of the impacts of his anger, the impacts of his destructive aura and the impacts on Earth because of Clarence.

If Clarence was not blinded by his anger and urge to improve his power, the evidence that he just destroyed an entire planet from months of training would have acted as a warning to avoid returning to Earth. However, so oblivious to the destruction around him was Clarence that his fixated thinking of returning home to Earth overrode any obvious evidence that this was a bad idea.

Clarence arrives on Earth then floats to Lackyer Vale. The town where he was once regarded as one of the most respected citizens, until Bob changed this forever.

Aware that his power has increased, although somehow still oblivious to the level it had increased; Clarence decides to visit the hill he had trained on. He decides he will visit this location one last time, say his goodbyes to Lackyer Vale and Earth and then leave to pursue Bob.

Clarence is Officially Missing

The day after the events of Bob's interaction with Clarence he is due for the weekly meeting. When he doesn't show to work his colleagues become worried. Clarence had never missed a meeting in his long career and as such, this was very out of character. His colleagues attempt to call him multiple times, but no one answers. They then perform a safety check, and no one answers the door or appears to be home. They attempt knocking and ringing his doorbell, but after waiting fifteen minutes on site, they return to the police station.

The town's police officers and Clarence's new boss are worried about Clarence. The new boss then calls the area manager. The new boss explains the situation and is given permission to enter Clarence's residence under suspicion of harm.

Two officers are sent to Clarence's residence. They spend half an hour inside his residence looking for clues about where Clarence might be, but they notice nothing odd. Nothing appears to be broken, there are no signs of struggle, and there are no signs of Clarence packing or leaving for good. The two officers then check Clarence's bedroom and again notice nothing legally odd.

However, they do notice bags upon bags of empty Whiskey and Bourbon bottles. Oddly though, the room doesn't stink of alcohol as one would expect as Clarence had apparently been washing each of the bottles before storing them in his room. The large quantity of empty alcohol bottles comes as a large shock to these officers. They knew that Clarence had lost his rank because of previous behaviours, and they knew that Clarence had returned to work as an officer.

Despite all of this, the officers still believed in Clarence's ability at work as he still seemed motivated. As such, they did not expect to see this amount of alcohol in his bedroom, suggesting that he was a functioning alcoholic.

The officers take notes and photos of the bottles and report their findings to their boss when they return to the station. The boss agrees that there is something odd about all of this and decides to discuss these findings with the area manager. After hearing about the alcohol found in Clarence's bedroom, the area manager than decides to visit Clarence's residence themselves to investigate further.

The next day the area manager arrives in town and picks up the two officers who had already been to Clarence's residence and they return together to the residence. They enter Clarence's residence and again check the area. The area manager acknowledges that everything seems to be fine with no signs of struggle.

However, the area manager eventually notices some odd faint red markings on the floor and the ceiling in Clarence's room. They notice that these red markings appear to be a type of burn and appear to be almost exactly in line with each other, with the ceiling circle and the floor circle appearing to make an invisible cylinder. Not knowing what this means, but fearing the worse, the area manager makes Clarence's residence a crime scene and calls the nearest forensic unit.

The two officers then start spouting theories about what the marks could mean. Could they just be alcohol marks, could Clarence have gone mad and become part of a cult, was Clarence secretly an art lover of circles? The area manager stops the officers' nonsense.

They then call the forensic unit from the nearest large town and wait in their office for the forensic unit to arrive.

Several days later forensic units from the nearest large town arrive and complete a thorough investigation. They check Clarence's online records, speak with almost the entire town, and by the end of the investigation, they had almost emptied Clarence's residence in search of evidence. They find nothing.

A missing person's notice is placed in the news, local newspaper and posters are placed around town. No one thinks to check the far side of the town's hill. Nobody knows anything about what has happened, so after two weeks of no new updates, Clarence is declared missing and deceased.

The town holds a public funeral with most of the town attending. The town is in mourning with many of the older members of the town finding it difficult to return to their normal work duties for several days. Clarence is given a full public police funeral. At Clarence's funeral many photos of Clarence and his police achievements are shared, and the local town hall is renamed in his honour. Clarence is now, officially deceased.

Lackper Vale Times

Beloved Police Officer Dead

After many weeks of searching for Clarence, we regret to inform the public that our beloved police officer Clarence has been declared deceased. He will be missed by all. He will be celebrated at the town's annual event.

good news for neighbouring Mongolia, a barren moose-wasteland whose inhabitents nonetheless have an insatiable desire for the creatures. The increase in Beijing-Ulanbataar trade is anticipated to relieve pressure on the relatively strained Russian suppliers, but increase Mongolia's imbalance of trade with its larger neighbour.

Historically the only competitor to China in the far eastern moose markets has been Singapore but the

Months after Clarence's official disappearance, and weeks after Clarence himself left Earth, more tourists are walking the town's hill. They notice a lot of damage from a distance towards what seems like the base of the hill. As it appears dangerous to investigate further, they call the police and share what they have found. The town's police chief arrives personally, to inspect. Once there, the police chief notices something very odd and calls for assistance, with the majority of the town's police officers arriving. They all travel down the hill and notice that everything seems to be dead, not burnt but dead.

There is no evidence of regrowth in vegetation, and it appears that someone had poisoned the entire area. The air itself is also more difficult to breathe, but no one is sure why. Eventually, one of the police officers' notices that there is a large gaping hole in the side of the hill which is not explained by the theory of poisoning.

The police chief enters the cave and finds red marks in the cave. They call the area manager to inspect. Once there the area manager is shocked to see these same markings again and confirms that the same markings were found months ago on the floor and ceiling of Clarence's room. The ones in the cave appear to be the same but appear to be more intense in their red colour.

All the new information gets added to Clarence's cold case file, and an official story is placed in the town's newspaper to explain the damage to the hill and its subsequent lack of safety – "an odd geographic occurrence, has caused the town's hill to cave in, leading to chemical runoff from the surrounding farms impacting the base of the hill. This has led to immense damage to the surrounding vegetation including the destruction of tree roots that were supporting the soil. As such the far side of the hill is now closed until further notice".

Despite the official story sounding somewhat convincing, almost no one in the town believes the official notice, but no one knows what to believe. Fuelled by bits of information shared by some of the junior officers, gossip circles around for several months.

Clarence is still officially deceased, but now some people are curious about what happened, leading to a myriad of conspiracy theories. The two main conspiracy theories circulating are that "he was abducted by Aliens just like Bob had been all those years ago" (although no one actually knew that Bob had been abducted by aliens) and "I heard that they found lots of whiskey in his room, and a ritual circle on his floor, maybe he just left and joined a cult".

Eventually, the town seems to collectively move on, at least officially.

Clarence Pure Anger

Several months after the hill damage had been investigated by the police, Calrence arrives back on Earth.

Clarence returns to the hill on Earth to say goodbye to his hometown. However, once he arrives, he sees police tape everywhere, although the tape is quickly vaporised soon after his landing. On Clarence's entry into Earth, he had again destroyed parts of the atmosphere and several satellites, all of which Clarence hasn't noticed. Clarence is unsure how he feels about being back on Earth in his hometown. As his power has grown, he feels he is becoming less human and feels this to be a positive.

Luckily, or unluckily, on the day that Clarence arrives back on Earth he witnesses a local news report showing photos of the Lackyer Vale's favourite members past and present, in a day of celebration. This celebration had started fifteen years ago in response to the town's declining morale. Local members had noticed that following a series of deaths from heart attacks, the town had felt collectively depressed. As such senior members had decided to celebrate the towns people past and present. Clarence had previously been celebrated as the town's police chief. The report Clarence is now witnessing discusses in detail all the people that helped to make this town great.

Instead of the report calming Clarence and making him feel wanted and appreciated it has the opposite effect. Seeing his photo in the news in a general police officer's uniform instead of the higher rank he once held, increases his anger regarding his thoughts of Bob. Clarence's care for his town, and care for human life in general begins to disappear as his anger for Bob continues to grow. To Clarence, it was Bob's fault those photos showed Clarence in a general officer uniform instead of the higher rank that he had worked so hard for so many years to achieve. His identity as human almost disappears.

Following months of training on Earth followed by the months of training on Venus, Clarence feels he has mastered his new form. Clarence now has multiple powers and abilities. He is able to vaporise objects by choice regardless of distance or size, he has a natural aura that vaporises anything that comes within several hundred metres of him. Clarence no longer needs to worry about phasing when travelling as he destroys anything in his way, with the atomic structure of anything within his aura having its' electronic charge destroyed. This is a natural byproduct of his new powers, and it means that he can travel at immense speeds by destroying energy around him at all times.

Clarence is now almost able to bend distance to his will through the destruction of energy, almost folding both space and time.

Clarence looks down below himself where the top of the hill was before he arrived back on Earth. Below him now lays nothing. The hill itself has been vaporised and is almost the same height of the surrounding roads. Seeing this and combined with the anger for Bob Clarence begins to believe himself to now be a god. He doesn't think that he is the god, or the only god in existence, but now feels that he is a god, nonetheless.

Instead of his training helping him find peace, instead of the town's celebration helping him feel wanted, it has increased his anger and hatred towards Bob. The angrier Clarence becomes, the more powerful he becomes, and the redder his being becomes. Eventually after months of training he has started to evolve even further than before.

Clarence becomes so angry he screams and grows in power further. His screams destroy several roads leading to where the town's hill had previously stood, and the sound of his scream can be heard for miles, stopping the town's celebrations. Everyone at the celebration stops and looks towards where the sound has come from. Several people notice a large red being with a cyclonic like aura. As Clarence's primary power is to destroy energy, it is impossible for the human eye to make a clear image out of what they see.

Losing perhaps the last of his humanity and related values and the last of his care for human life, Clarence becomes a being of pure anger with only one goal in mind, destroying Bob once and for all including destroying anything that stands in his way. He now appears as a large red being, Clarence's shape and form is rather fluid, but the angrier Clarence becomes the more solid and humanoid looking he becomes at the centre. He is now always surrounded by an aura that appears as a cyclone or hurricane does on a weather forecast, immense and spinning.

Clarence has not had the need for breathing, toileting or eating for a long time now, and is now fuelled and driven solely by anger. The spectrum of anger related emotions all become fuel for him. The understanding, caring, hardworking Clarence that many of Lackyer Vale had grown to love and look up to, has now completely disappeared.

Clarence now feels ready, ready to destroy Bob. There are no thoughts about life after Bob's destruction. Clarence only focuses on destroying Bob.

The town never recovers from Clarence's
destruction, and we will soon find out
that neither does life on Earth.

Clarence is Ready

Unknown to Bob, during his travels he has left a slight energy trail that most beings and technologies would not be able to read. Clarence is unlike anything that had come before, Clarence is able to follow the slight energy trail.

Clarence floats above Earth to begin his journey of revenge and destruction. Since Clarence's recent ascensions, he is vaguely able to read this trail to have a rough idea regarding Bob's travel direction, Clarence notices a slight energy trail heading away from the solar system, and perhaps towards the centre of the Milky Way galaxy. Clarence begins traversing the solar system on the lookout for Bob.

Initially, Clarence travels slowly. Whilst he had mastered his powers on Earth, his initial trip through the centre of the Earth taught him he should master his new powers in new environments. His time on Venus helped improve his destructive ability, but he was still getting used to the folding of space and time. Clarence spends several weeks travelling towards Bob, making adjustments for the different solar systems. As he continues understanding his powers, he continues growing stronger as the vaporising aura surrounding increases in magnitude. He does not pay attention to any destruction being left behind him as after Clarence leaves Earth, he leaves the last tiny part of his humanity behind.

When Clarence left Earth with his aura constantly surrounding him, accidental destruction happens. He had previously accidently destroyed Lackyer Vale's largest hill just by being above it. Now as Clarence leaves Earth, his aura destroys parts of the earth's atmosphere at each layer (including the troposphere, stratosphere, mesosphere and thermosphere). His aura destroys satellites needed for modern communication. His aura destroys energy involved in Earth's moon's gravitational travels and destroys various asteroids.

Unknown to Clarence, he has accidently ensured the destruction of the Earth.

A week after he has left Earth's solar system the inhabitants of Earth begin to suffer. The first five days prior to the end of the world as we know it, scientists attempted to explain to the politicians and the general public that this was not normal and that something drastic had to be done. However, no one with power, position or money officially listened to the scientists and continued focusing on their own goals. The billionaires and their friends built exclusive bunkers for their own protection in secret as the warnings were listened to, but the welfare of humanity was not as important as self-preservation.

This inaction by those in positions of power and money, combined with Clarence's destructive aura, led to mass destruction. On the seventh day after Clarence had left Earth, the sun's radiation, various asteroids, the change of the moon's rotation around the Earth, the volcanic activity triggered by plate tectonic shifts that were triggered by the moon and the massive earthquakes and tsunamis that were also triggered by the moon, destroy almost all life and humanity in general on Earth.

Noone on Earth knew what caused the damage, and most did not have time to respond to the damage. Those who did have the time but did not have the power to do anything chose to ignore the warnings and instead enjoy the last bits of their lives.

On the final day of chaos, the best and the worst of humanity was evident for all to experience. The remaining humans are forced underground with an estimated five percent of humanity still remaining.

For the next thousand years humans managed to cling on to surviving. However, as has happened across most of human history this clinging to survival led to wars. The limited resources led to in-fighting. This in turn, led to the final destruction of the human race via the use of the remaining nuclear arsenal in an act of final desperation.

Lackyer Vale is no more.

Humanity is no more.

Life on Earth is no more?

Bob Leaves Sodatsu

The king's guards inform the king that Zion urgently needs him. Neo-Ronin quickly arrives with his guards to Zion's location. He is able to calm Zion enough to enquire what is wrong. Zion points towards where Jay's grave previously stood.

Bob is now caught by the king and Zion messing with Jay's remains. Zion is angry and the king asks some of his guards to take Zion someplace quiet. Meanwhile, the king teleports with two of his guards to where Bob was floating. The king is also enraged but keeps a calm exterior. He asks Bob why he destroyed Jay's grave.

Bob then tells the king about his relationship with Jay and how Jay was with child before the civil war. Bob explains that Zion's accusation regarding the prince is correct, in that prince Neon targeted Jay on the battlefield in attempt to weaken Bob. Bob tells the king that he had returned to Sodatsu with the hope of reviving Jay after his recent improvements regarding his powers and potential further evolution.

The king now allows his emotions to be shown to Bob. The king is horrified that Bob thought he could and should bring back a deceased being. The king explains that this is against everything he believes in and goes against most if not all ideas of balance. The king is also angered, feeling betrayed by Bob's deceit. The king tells Bob that he must be losing his grip with what life and death means.

The king informs Bob that he must now regrettably banish Bob from Sodatsu for life. Bob is not allowed to return and if Bob ever returns, he will be treated as an enemy and targeted with lethal force. The king warns Bob that they had already begun improvements in their technological capabilities regarding combating pure energy forms, as many Sodatsu beings saw Bob's raw power and were frightened. The king warns Bob, that despite his improved powers, it is not worth the risk for Bob to engage in combat with his people.

Bob is saddened further but understands and then agrees to leave Sodatsu to travel amongst the various galaxies. Bob promises to never return to Sodatsu, and requests the king apologise to Zion on his behalf. Before Bob leaves, he asks if the king has a way of storing immense energy as Bob wishes to leave a part of himself on the planet as an apology.

King Neo-Ronin remembers his son's light box and orders it be brought to him. Soon after the light box arrives, Bob transfers a small fraction of his power into the light box. The light box appears to react, and almost become sentient itself, before becoming quiet again. The light box is sent to Zion's work area for future study.

Bob hopes that his power will show the king and Zion he is sorry and is a token of faith. Bob advises the king that he believes the energy in the light box could be used as a weapon against Bob once Sodatsu's scientists had time to run experiments, should Bob ever return. Bob also hopes the tiny part of his power remaining on Sodatsu will help him feel closer to Jay and help keep the memory of Jay and Bob alive for himself and for Sodatsu.

Just as Bob is about to leave Sodatsu forever, the king remembers one more thing. His scientists had found that multiversal theory might be more real than first thought. The king shares that his scientists believe there are two other beings of immense power moving towards the centre of the galaxy. The scientists initially thought their data and interpretations were wrong, and then they thought it must have been Bob. However, they had the same readings while Bob was on Sodatsu. The king tells Bob that he is sharing this information as he believes that if Bob really is sorry for what he has done, that once he has travelled through space, he should eventually confront these two new beings. Bob thanks the king for this new information, apologises once more, then leaves.

Once Bob leaves Sodatsu, he travels as he said he would throughout space, floating almost aimlessly. Bob deduces that one of the two powerful beings must be Clarence, but he is unsure what the third would be. Since space is so massive, and if multiversal theory is in fact a reality, it would be of no use for Bob to look for the other energy being. Bob decides that he will travel some more and when he is ready, he might travel back towards Earth to see if his hunch about Clarence is correct.

During Bob's travels he has slowly been growing in energy potential, becoming more energy dense each time he passes through a black hole. Every time he passes through a black hole, he feels different.

Bob's powers have been growing but instead of increasing in size, he continued to become denser. By the time he would meet up with Clarence, Bob would be smaller than the average human, but denser than any Neutron star known in the universe. He begins to become aware of an interruption in the flow of energy but cannot explain this. He then deduces that this must be the third powerful being that the Sodatsu scientists had readings of but couldn't understand.

Based on Bob's continuing growth in power, he feels there will become a time that he will be able to fathom this third being but for now, he feels it would be a waste of his time and effort.

For now, Bob continues his slow travels almost aimlessly, through the various solar systems, galaxies and black holes. With his increasing density, his speed of travel has also increased allowing him to travel vast distances in seconds. Bob continues exploring and also attempts to explore the outermost parts of the universe but finds this difficult as he never finds what he feels is the edge of the universe. Eventually, he decides to go back towards the centre of the known universe and float around for a while, eventually stopping at the Abell galaxy.

Time is meaningless to Bob but eventually he hears something that gets his attention when he exits the black hole in the 'Abell 1835 IR1916' galaxy. "I have finally found you and it is your time to cease existing". Before he turns

around, he feels that the energy balance
in the universe around him has just
changed for the worse.

Clarence's Travels

Thanks to Clarence's training and understanding of his powers, he has continued to change. He has been changing and becoming larger and redder, although keeping a translucent-like appearance. Clarence is embracing his increases in size and power.

Clarence's size continued to grow and begins to grow at a rapid pace. By the time Clarence finds Bob, he will be at least the size of Earth's solar system, possibly much larger. Every time Clarence destroyed energy either from his aura or by his choice, the energy from the destroyed matter became part of him. The more energy the destroyed object had, the quicker Clarence's size and power grew.

Clarence had continued following the feint green energy trail left by Bob. Clarence had continued destroying solar systems and any surrounding matter whilst following the trail.

Clarence was now becoming so powerful he was able to destroy blackholes just by travelling near or through them. Every time Clarence destroyed a black hole the universe appeared to shrink. Instead of the expanding universe human scientists had been theorising, Clarence's power began sucking energy from the universe itself.

By the time he met Bob he was enormous. Light itself could no longer escape Clarence's vaporising aura. Green energy emitting lights began disappearing at a fast rate, furthering empowering Clarence's view about himself.

Eventually, Clarence follows Bob's energy trail to a galaxy known on Earth as 'Abell 1835 IR1916' galaxy. The energy trail seems to disappear. Possibly because of Clarence's enormous power destroying all energy, or possibly because Bob had travelled through this way a long time ago. Either way this does not suit Clarence. Initially Clarence is annoyed.

However, he then decides to wait here, and he focuses on further strengthening himself. For the first time since he ascended from a weak human body, he had become bored. His power was becoming so large and vaporising and absorbing so much energy that maintaining his form began to become difficult. Even thinking about Bob and everything Bob had done to him was having less impact. Just as Clarence felt that he might fall apart from the centre something happens.

Clarence sees something in the distance. Clarence begins to travel towards the oddity as it looks like a denser version of Bob in the distance.

Bob is emitting the brightest, most intense green Clarence has ever experienced. It is far more intense than any blackhole or sun that Clarence has destroyed so far. It is so intense that not even Clarence's vaporising aura could destroy the green light it was emitting.

Once there, Clarence realises this is in fact a smaller Bob. Clarence yells out to Bob. Except instead of a yell, the sound created by Clarence seems to bounce until it reaches Bob. The sound powered by Clarence's pure anger being and his vaporising aura, is heard by the nearest universes with many solar systems being destroyed as a side effect.

Supernatural Ending Part One – Bob vs Clarence One Last Time

Bob is now rather small, with an approximate height of one and a half metres. He is super dense and is beginning to have his own aura made of energy including temperature and light.

Bob finally hears Clarence's call and turns around expecting to see a human sized red being. Instead, Bob sees a being unfathomable to a normal human brain, but best explained by the cyclone analogy, but at a size almost as large as the Milky Way Galaxy. Bob is surprised by the size and potential power for destruction Clarence now holds. This will be a fight between a giant beyond measure and a dot.

After an unknown amount of time Clarence has finally found Bob. This meeting not only leads to a giant battle but leads to a battle so massive it will forever change all of existence in this universe and the rest. Bob and his super condensed energy form vs Clarence's enormous red chemical energy being, fuelled by emotions and strengthened by destruction.

The battle takes place at the approximate halfway point between the Milky Way galaxy and the Jades Galaxy, near the black hole of the 'Abell 1835 IR1916' galaxy.

Initially Bob is taken back by the sheer magnitude and magnificence of Clarence's new form. If Clarence wasn't here to kill Bob, it would have been the best thing Bob had ever witnessed, but the murder context of the meeting changes how Bob feels about Clarence's enormous size. Bob feels that he is no longer fighting for his own survival but is now fighting for the survival of any remaining living lifeform including all of Sodatsu, with thoughts about Earth and his parents no longer available to him. Bob feels that at least if he can stop Clarence, he might be honouring Jay's memory, in his own way.

Despite this, Bob attempts one last time to avoid a fight. Bob initially attempts to talk with Clarence about how change can improve us and how we can use change for the betterment of lower lifeforms. Clarence does not care for words. Clarence no longer holds value for anything other than himself.

When talking fails Bob decides to flee and attempt to trap Clarence, although he has still not worked out how. However, Clarence has grown exponentially since their last meeting and is now strong enough to stop Bob from fleeing by utilising the vaporising aura's power to pull Bob towards himself. Bob instead uses his power to remain in place.

Clarence begins the battle by destroying all the remaining matter around Bob. Bob notices the remaining planets, suns, asteroids, and even the closest blackhole seem to vaporise or fall apart. The universe as Bob knew it, seems to have been partially destroyed and folding in on itself.

Clarence laughs at Bob declaring himself a god, a god of war and destruction, perhaps even the one and only god ever in existence. Clarence begins aiming his powers of destruction towards Bob. After multiple attempts to destroy Bob, nothing appears to be happening. Clarence is annoyed that Bob is still alive and resisting his attacks. Bob's new super condensed form is initially able to hold Clarence's attacks at bay.

Eventually, Bob realises that he will need to go on the offensive. Bob attempts to shoot parts of himself at Clarence but this does nothing except increase Clarence's power which in turn leads to Clarence laughing at Bob. Bob then decides to focus all of his energy powers towards Clarence attempting to disrupt and destroy Clarence's new form but to no avail. Again, Clarence only laughs at Bob's feeble attempts. There is no energy or matter around Bob that he can use to increase his strength or distract Clarence. His energy attacks have failed. Bob feels he has failed himself, all remaining lifeforms and most importantly feels he has failed Jay.

Unknown to Clarence and Bob, their battle is so immense that the remaining universes begin losing solar systems. The boundaries between universes also begin shrinking allowing other powerful beings to travel more quickly between universes. With one such example being the powerful being the Sodatsu scientists had recorded data about, that led to Neo-Ronin's warning to Bob.

Bob has one more idea on how to destroy Clarence. If Bob can reduce his density further, whilst keeping or increasing his power, he might be able to engulf Clarence's new form, smothering Clarence's destructive abilities. Bob attempts to expand himself, however because of Clarence's powers of energy destruction, any attempt by Bob of reducing density only weakens Bob and empowers Clarences. There is nothing Bob can do. He has again failed. Bob then remembers that there is always one last option.

Bob deduces that a kamikaze option might be the only remaining option. Bob is no longer sure that he or Clarence are capable of dying or being destroyed. He does know that he has to try. Bob's new denser form allowed him to travel faster than he was previously capable of. He felt that if Clarence was capable of being destroyed, then Bob would be the only living being capable of doing so.

Bob, then increases his density so he now stands no more than one metre tall. His density is more power than all recorded neutron stars in existence combined. The intensity and brightness of the green light he is emitting, temporarily overloads Clarence's ability to visually interpret his environment. Bob then flies at Clarence as fast as he is capable.

Initially Clarence's natural aura of destruction slows Bob and even throws him to the side. Clarence did not know that it was possible to be blinded since his ascensions. Undeterred, Bob tries several more times, each time failing and each time Clarence outwardly gloating about his own raw power, whilst inwardly still being unable to see. For the first time in forever, Clarence has a feeling of fear as he does not like being blinded.

This feeling of fear weakens Clarence enough so that eventually Bob is able to travel faster than he had ever travelled before and hits Clarence in what would be the approximate centre point of Clarence's being. If a being could witness and understand the event, it would have appeared to be a bright green speck of dirt, changing into an even brighter green dot, entering a giant red fluid object.

Both Bob and Clarence are shocked. They appear to have merged. Bob representing energy and matter and Clarence representing raw emotion and anti-matter. They are unable to disentangle. Yet despite this forced merging, Clarence doesn't stop his attempts at destruction. He continues his attempt to destroy Bob, with no care about his own destruction. Bob is forced to defend and attempt to counterattack but is unable to do anything useful except defend.

The new combined form of Bob's super condensed energy form and Clarence's enormous chaotic anger fuelled form is different. When Bob's form entered Clarence's form, Clarence's aura began to disappear. Clarence became denser and Bob's form began to spread.

The new combined form of Bob and Clarence continues to grow but thin. Soon Clarence's previous centre of his being has grown to the size his aura previously was. Bob and Clarence are now an enormous being of all the colours possible, except for bright blue. They continue changing colours randomly and what feels like forever.

Their existence now represents a duality of the universe, with one of creation versus destruction.

Eventually, Bob and Clarence are both forced into an eternal cycle of attack and adaptation, locked in an endless cosmic struggle bound to each other for eternity. This endless fighting amongst their one singular merged being, begins to make changes, further evolving both Bob and Clarence.

After the equivalent of millions of Earth years passing, with Bob and Clarence fighting within themselves, a final form of evolution occurs. Both Clarence and Bob evolve to become an abstract concept of thought alone. Their colour changing has ceased and they are no longer visible to any known being or technology to ever exist. Neither being now has the ability to live without the other as they become reliant on each other's existence. They have become the abstract thought of duality itself. They have become the idea of balance.

They are now one being, eternally connected, and powered by thoughts of other beings. For them to find peace they would need to find a way to destroy reality itself. They continue their battle as abstract intertwined thoughts until near the end of the universe. Negative and destructive thoughts fuel Clarence's part of the existence and calming and positive thoughts fuel Bob's part of the existence. There are periods when Bob has the advantage and then there are periods where Clarence takes back the advantage. Further reinforcing a now ancient human idea of Yin and Yang.

Millions of Earth years have again occurred, but Bob and Clarence are completely unable to perceive time. They are now barely being stimulated from thought as most of the living beings of the universe capable of thought have died. They seem to drift as one for eternity, bound together but constantly at war. They continue their war, without knowledge as to why. They continue their fighting as an instinct, as a need for balance. Eventually, they begin to weaken as the last being capable of conscious thought dies somewhere in the universe.

However, before their destruction, before they are released from this eternity of war and balance, something odd occurs. They somehow manage to feel for the first time in a long time. They manage to feel a very odd and very powerful presence.

Supernatural Ending Part Two – A Third Joins

Bob and Clarence have now become one being. Just when they thought their abstract existence might finally be over, they feel for the first time in a long time. They feel something very odd. Bob now has no memories about Sodatsu nor about Earth. He has been fighting for so long now that his memories of life before the duality state, have now faded. Clarence also has no memories. He has no memories regarding why he hates Bob so much, he has been fighting for so long that memories have faded. Instead, Clarence's war with Bob has become a need rather than a goal of revenge.

During Bob and Clarence's battles the universe had begun shrinking at an alarming rate. The boundaries between universes had also been shrinking. This shrinking in distance attracted something. Something very powerful.

An even more abstract and illogical being far more powerful than Bob and Clarence's combined form arrives. The abstract form is unfathomable for lower forms, and it has been given many names. For simplicity purposes, this abstract and illogical being is known by lifeforms as 'Love' and has itself been drifting throughout the universes, it has travelled through various multiversal layers and seems to arrive in our own universe.

This being of Love contained immense power and had existed before known time. Whilst it was existing in a universe, it improved all the living organisms' ability to evolve together and work collectively. It would exist or move in a universe and then become almost bored of existing in a specific universe then just appear in the next. This being of Love contained an immense bright blue light, visible to any living creature. However, by the time this being of Love arrives in our universe all lifeforms capable of technology and creative thought have since died.

This third illogical and abstract being of Love, seems drawn to Bob and Clarence. It has an irresistible urge to be with Bob and Clarence. It seems to move towards them.

Time no longer exists in the traditional sense as it begins folding around this being of Love. This being of Love continues toward Bob and Clarence duality form. Despite Bob and Clarence being an abstract form themselves, this immense being of Love somehow manages to find and successfully merge with their abstract thought forms. Bob and Clarence's combined form no long feels anything. They are no longer at war with each other. They no longer seek to win.

Again, this combined form of Bob and Clarence feel. They feel the end is nearing. Bob attempts to release all of his energy and Clarence attempts the same, but to no avail. They are now merging with Love at a rapid rate. This being of Love has no goals, no thoughts, and just behaves based on its unexplainable urges.

Supernatural Ending Part Three – The Biggest Bang

The three have almost completely merged. The merging of the three most powerful, most abstract beings in the remaining multiverse creates an enormous bang. This initial explosion destroys the remainder of this universe and any other universes that the Love being had previously existed in. All is silent, all is black. Bob and Clarence are now fuelled by whatever is fuelling Love.

Then as if rewound and replayed, the explosion appears to reverse and repeat several times, with each replay of the explosion increasing in magnitude. Each explosion finding new universes to destroy including ones that Love had never visited. Each explosion increasing the power of this newly merged being.

After every possible universe seems to have been destroyed, something incredible happens. This super abstract being consisting of Bob, Clarence and Love, creates a final explosion that recreates the universes. Bob, Clarence and Love appear to be destroyed.

These new universes appear similar to our own with one major difference. This major difference involves a kind of emotional vacuum where love, hate, anger and emotions in general appear to not exist. All beings that would come after this final explosion would be driven by only survival and eventually after further evolution, only survival and logic. Emotions had appeared to be no more.

These beings of survival and logic were amazingly effective. Decisions were based on resource need. Survival strategies were subconsciously calculated on a cost/benefit analysis by the individual and by those in positions of power. Communication was primarily completed with numerical transactions with numbers being the dominant language across many species and cultures. This allowed for great civilisations to develop more quickly than they had in the original universes.

However, the logical and non-existent emotional drive for sharing meant that the need for resources eventually outweighed the benefits of sharing and this eventually led to many wars across galaxies and across universes. The almost cold like logical creatures had different values and ideas regarding resource seeking.

These different values lead to different cultural ideas about what life and death meant, with life and death now having less value, and resource accumulation having more value. It also meant ideas around health care and illness were based on the impact on resource gathering potential. Death, however, was still granted extra effort regarding language use, but only if the being had contributed their share of resources.

The occasional being experienced versions of emotions that no one understood and only saw as errors in logic. As such, these emotions were ignored or suppressed by the individual and the majority. Occasionally a being would have dreams of wonder and curiosity. However, if the person attempted to understand these or attempted to explain these to others, they were again seen as errors in logic and were strongly discouraged.

Many of these logical beings lived in small towns to improve efficiency. The idea of family was seen through a resource lens. When an adult had enough resources and wanted to increase their output, they would choose a partner who had a similar level of resources. Together they would then accept a short-term loss of resources for the potential of a long-term gain, with children often contributing resource gathering at a young age.

In this new universe there is an Earth-like planet, where humanoids are developing space travel and are almost ready to land on the nearest extraterrestrial satellite that orbits the planet. This satellite is known locally as 'The Cheese Moon' because the craters observed through the telescopes appeared to be similar to a famous cheese.

The leader of the space program has an affinity with anything electricity related, both with his inventions and oddly with his biology. He has been able to invent most of the equipment this new mission will be using. The leader of the space program has kept his biological affinity to electricity a secret from his friends, colleagues and family.

He wants to be known as the greatest Astronaut of all time and doesn't want to jeopardise this. He is already famous and is well off resource wise. He also understands that should anyone find out about his electricity affinity, the only logical decision would be to run scientific experiments on him which would destroy his ability to visit The Cheese Moon. He will not let this happen.

When he dies, he wants his grave head to read "Here lies Neo Bob Clarence Smith, the greatest Astronaut the world has seen, and the most active resource gathering husband and father a family could ever benefit from".

The End?

P.S. Neo Bob Clarence Smith

What if Love, Hate, and emotions in general weren't truly erased and were instead waiting for the right spark?

Neo Bob or Smithy as his friends call him had always had the affinity for electricity for as long as he could remember. As a child he understood technology the same way most people understood numbers or each other. Smithy had difficulty connecting socially with his peers as he found their focus on raw numbers boring and repetitive. As such Smithy spent most of his childhood alone tweaking his parents' technology and improving its effectiveness. His parents never understood how Smithy did this, but they benefited from the resource efficiency so they encouraged Smithy as much as they could.

Also unknown to his parents were Smithy's other differences. The first of which were his dreams. To the best of Smithy's knowledge, his peers and family members rarely had these things called dreams, and if they did, they were focused on numbers and resource gathering for the individual and small group benefit. Smithy's dreams were not like these.

Smithy had dreams about giant green three-armed aliens who could move vast distances with ease and who had energy type powers. He had dreams about a being that was capable of flying through space without the need for technology whilst simultaneously increasing in power and reducing in size. He had dreams about a giant red being that was surrounded by a cyclone that seemed to destroy everything it came close to. He even had dreams about a giant blue being that spread this virus type thing that made other lifeforms have this odd thing called feelings.

Of all of Smithy's dreams, this odd thing known as feelings was the most familiar to him. Noone else known to Smithy could comprehend what feelings were. On multiple occasions he had attempted to explain this to teachers or parents or peers and was either faulted for his faulty logic or bullied by his peers. Over time, Smithy learnt to hide this experience known as feelings and he also learnt that his differences would not be supported, so he would have to hide his other differences as well.

The other dream about the green beings with energy powers also resonated with Smithy. He didn't know how to control his powers as a child but felt the dreams gave him a sense of calm regarding his power.

The second difference Smithy experienced involved his energy affinity.

As mentioned, he could communicate with the technology around him with ease, if it used electricity. He could communicate via thought and touch alone to improve its effectiveness. However, his ability to improve technology also often brought up his other difference of feelings, especially around something he called emptiness.

Smithy felt that this emptiness was like a hole that needed filling with resources. Instead of physical resources though, Smithy had to understand what he needed so he could fill his emptiness feeling. As Smithy grew older, he began communicating with living things by thought and touch alone.

His electrical affinity had grown in complexity and power. He could still improve technology through touch and thought alone, but now he could influence living things including plants, animals and eventually his peers.

Luckily for his peers, his family, and others of his species, Smithy also had another feeling thing he called "being kind". He rarely used his power to manipulate his peers, and when he did, he did so for what he felt was "the greater good".

Smithy's understanding of himself, combined with him almost mastering his powers of electrical affinity and feelings, allowed him to flourish in his chosen fields. However, there was something within him that drove him to want to explore beyond his planet.

Many of his science peers had attempted to explain The Cheese Moon that appeared to move around his planet, and he wanted to explore this in person. He dedicated many years to mastering his affinity and focusing it on space travel and exploration. Strangely, whenever he had a breakthrough with the space technologies, it would be followed by dreams of the giant three-armed aliens curving their lips into what Smithy had now called smiling.

There was also an unknown side-effect of Smithy's powers. Every being he had ever touched had their genome change a tiny amount, currently immeasurable by their technology, but known to us humans as epigenetics. Smithy was unaware that his powers acted like a virus. This virus had an urge of its own to live and would seek new hosts whenever Smithy touched technology or living lifeforms including his peers and family.

Unknown to everyone, this virus was influencing and manipulating technology and genomes so that it might live. This virus had a type of hive sentience which grew stronger the more things Smithy touched. The hive like sentience was easily able to communicate via energy and this would be explained by our modern humans as quantum mechanics and energy transfer; but to everyone on Smithy's world this knowledge was yet to be discovered.

When Smithy wasn't focusing on space, he was focusing on providing for his new love interest JJ. JJ always had some unknown chemical urge to be near Smithy and Smithy always wanted to be with JJ. Smithy promised himself he would never use his powers to influence JJ. After being together for many years, and after seeing Smithy's ability to provide ample resources, JJ and Smithy had their first child named Jessie Jay.

Unknown to JJ and Smithy, they had just accidently started or perhaps reinforced, a new branch of evolution. As Jessie Jay grew up it became clear to JJ, Smithy and their families that there was something very different about Jessie Jay. However, unlike his parents, childhood peers and childhood teachers, Smithy tried his best to ensure Jessie Jay had all the support they needed to flourish. The virus that no one knew about had also decided to make Jessie Jay it's new host. This different something in Jessie Jay would change the lives of all living lifeforms forever.

With Smithy's support and her own drive, Jessie Jay became a very successful astronaut in their own right. And after several years as an astronaut, she decided to have children with her astronaut colleague. Jessie Jay and her colleague had several children of their own, who in turn had several children of their own. Twenty generations later, the posterity of Jessie Jay begins to explore the universe.

One of the posterities leads an exhibition into deep space to investigate closer, the nearest blackhole and its impact on energy. Unfortunately, they are sucked into the black hole and are never seen again. This adult was known by his friends and family as Bob.

Alternate Ending 1? Part One – D.I.D Response

Bob wakes in the hospital after being hit in the head by the unknown object. His meat abattoir colleague found him on the ground and called the ambulance. After two days in hospital Bob can leave and return home. Bob returns to living with Leo Dafishy. Initially, Bob feels that he is okay and doesn't notice anything different about himself.

However, once Bob is home, he begins to have conversations with himself from multiple different perspectives. Bob has experienced a lot of traumas in his life predominantly in his childhood. He also experienced a lot of attachment trauma as his parents were not helpful regarding most of his difficulties. Bob had always wanted to escape his hometown, but his own anxieties meant that this was very unlikely. Unknown to Bob his previous life traumas, the stress from his mundane life, his want to escape and the final hit to the head had combined and caused a severe trauma response leading to multiple personality constructs known as identities.

Each of these identities serve a function and a representation of various aspects of Bob as a person and his goals and desires. Bob's first alternative identity is known as Clarence. Clarence is a hardworking older male and focuses on the job. Clarence has no other hobbies, and his identity is tied up with his work. Clarence always hated injustice and always wanted to be a police officer as a child. After Bob's recent accident, whenever he is struggling at work Clarence takes over.

Jessie is a shy gender-neutral person whose childhood was filled with abuse and drug use. Jessie is very quiet but fancies themselves as a puzzle connoisseur. When Bob's boredom becomes unbearable at home or in general, Jessies takes control purchasing puzzles or participating in online puzzle competitions.

Zion is a scientist and science genius and loves performing experiments. Bob had always enjoyed some of the sciences at school but never pursued this because of the academic and social pressures he observed from other science loving students. Even as an adult he had kept his interest in science. Whenever Bob has left over liquids such as cola and he is bored, Zion takes over performing multiple experiments with cola and other chemicals and ingredients in the house.

Neon is an overconfident young male who thinks he is an actor and athlete. There are several younger female colleagues at the meatworks that Bob has never spoken with. He has avoided them like everyone else. However, whenever he sees one particular female colleague his eyes fixate on her. Occasionally, this has led to Neon taking over Bob's actions.

Neo-Ronin is a political leader and pacifist. He rarely shows himself. Some days at work where it has been particularly busy, and the amount of coagulated animal blood has begun covering Bob more than usual, Neo-Ronin takes over. Neo-Ronin begins exclaiming veganism as the only safe alternative and attempts to have support from Bob's colleagues at the meat abattoirs.

Steve is a drug user and self-proclaimed numbers savant. Occasionally when Bob is at home, he watches TV and sees gambling advertisements. Occasionally when Bob sees these advertisements it triggers Steve. Steve will then take over and make some calls.

Laura is a highly successful and powerful businesswoman. Bob does not understand fashion and sees no reason to spend money on new fashion. He also does not understand the impracticality of women's fashion. Occasionally, when Bob goes clothes shopping and feels pressured by the salesperson, Laura takes over and has an ability to know what the most expensive fashion item in the store is and an urge to purchase it.

Throughout all of these identities Bob is still the primary or the core identity. When the other identities take over, Bob has a third person view of the events unfolding. He is unable to wrestle back control over his brain and body but is able to observe every detail. This can often lead to him feeling powerless during the other identities and feeling powerless when he resumes control. Bob would love to have full control back over his functioning but does not know who to speak with about his current difficulties.

Bob never consciously chooses which identity takes over, furthering his sense of powerlessness, but the identity always serves its purpose in the moment. When the identity feels it has completed its purpose, Bob will suddenly be given control again, often at the worst possible time. Eventually, the impact of these identities begins negatively effecting Bob's life leading to him being forcibly taken to a mental health hospital.

Alternate Ending 1? Part Two – D.I.D Functioning Impact

Bob has now been experiencing undiagnosed 'Dissociative Identity Disorder' now for several months, and he is starting to lose the last bit of control he had left.

On a particularly cold day outside, Bob is feeling a lot of joint pain in his shoulders and wrists. This puts him in a lower than usual mood. He arrives to work and sees the factory line is already filled with cattle ready for production. The 'Kill Floor' had worked overtime last night meaning that the 'Boning Room Floor' where Bob worked had a lot more work than usual. Towards the end of the day, a colleague of Bob says something that Bob takes personally. This then triggers Neo-Ronin.

Neo-Ronin looks down at himself and notices he is covered in more coagulated blood than he has ever seen. This infuriates him and fills him with confidence to let the whole chain, perhaps even the whole room know. He stands on the cutting table causing the chains to be stopped. Neo-Ronin then beings an impassioned speech about animal rights and how veganism is the way of the future.

Initially many of Bob's colleagues are shocked that this quiet person is making a loud statement, and that Bob is acting as someone else completely different, almost like he was in a movie. Several minutes after this, many of Bob's colleagues begin laughing at him and eventually after fifteen minutes of interruption, security is called, and they take Bob away. As Neo-Ronin has almost reached the office, Bob takes back over. Bob attempts to explain what happened but the manager is not hearing it. Bob is sent home and given a written warning.

A month after the big event involving Neo-Ronin, work has started becoming whelming for Bob. He has already received a written warning, and since the Neo-Ronin speech event, his colleagues have continued to increase their teasing towards Bob. As such Clarence is beginning to take over more often. Initially, this increases Bob's cutting speed, and he is smashing the daily work goals. Eventually though, Bob is tired from work and the recent increase in speed, the amount of constant bullying and the lack of response from the foreman towards Bob triggers the largest Clarence take over. Clarence takes over at the start of a shift and argues with the foreman about workplace safety violations from his colleagues and the foreman himself.

Bob's colleagues again witness a massive change from Bob. His posture seems to have changed dramatically, he appears to be standing in a form of fighting stance, and his arm and hand gestures are purposeful and menacing. The foreman has worked in the meat abattoirs for over thirty years and does not care what his worker is telling him. The foreman responds aggressively which only triggers Clarence's response more. Clarence begins to yell at the foreman highlighting the foreman's personal vulnerabilities such as his lack of height.

This then leads to the foreman pushing Bob, and Clarence returns with a right hook. Once the foreman picks himself off the ground, Bob is fired on the spot. He is told to hand in his uniform including his knives, knife belt, and boots. As Bob reaches the washdown room, he again takes back control over his body. He is upset about losing the only job he was good at and decides to go shopping since he feels his normal TV use and speaking with Leo Dafishy might not be enough to distract him.

Bob stops to fuel his car and half an hour later he arrives at the local shopping corner. He goes to the only clothing store in Lackyer Vale to look for new trousers, preferrable ones with pockets. Bob is taking his time looking through the various trouser options when the salesperson becomes inpatient and asks Bob for the third time in twenty minutes if they can assist Bob with anything. Bob has just lost his job, has a sore hand and the pressure from the salesperson causes him to snap, again. Laura takes over.

Laura tells the salesperson they are fine thank you and the salesperson is taken back by the change in voice pitch and body demeanour. The salesperson becomes uncomfortable and leaves the customer alone. Laura then stops looking at the trouser section and instead chooses an expensive dress. The dress is brightly coloured and has a matching hat. Laura then goes to pay for the items but accidently drops the bank card. Just as Laura is bending over to collect the card from the floor Bob suddenly takes back over. He sees what is in his hands, freaks out and then runs out of the shop. He had forgotten to drop the items initially and so as he attempted to run out of the shop he trips over the dress and the hat as they fall onto his legs and under his feet. The salesperson then bans Bob from entering the shop again.

Bob now just wants to cry. He rushes to his car, slides down the driver's seat, turns up the radio and cries. Bob has not cried for many years, but the last several months have been the most difficult in his life. He does not understand what is happening. In Lackyer Vale no one talks about mental health, everyone just takes a teaspoon of cement and hardens up. This approach combined with complete avoidance of his problems and of other people has worked well for Bob until now. Eventually, the crying helps to calm his nerves, and Bob chooses to go to the local bakery, subconsciously to buy the sweetest, unhealthiest item they have. Bob hasn't eaten since the morning and is now feeling famished.

Once Bob arrives there, he sees two of his female former colleagues. The colleague he has found attractive for many years is there. Because of the intense emotional rollercoaster of a day Bob has experienced, upon seeing his female former colleague, Neon takes over.

Bob's posture again changes from the hunched shoulders to his shoulders being drawn back and his chest out. Neon walks over to the former colleagues and attempts to flirt with them. Bob has not been home since his work shift, and by this stage the stagnant blood smell has worsened. His former colleagues are not interested and have found Bob to be even more weird the last few months then they had ever thought before. This combined with the recent work events and Bob's smell leads to the former colleague Bob found most attractive, ridiculing him. Neon does not notice the insults and attempts the flirting again. Neon moves in closer towards the former colleague until she screams at him. A large male bystander who also happens to work on the farms, taps Bob on the shoulder. Neon turns around and is punched in the face.

Bob takes back over as he is falling towards the ground. He stands up, attempts an apology, and again runs to his car.

Bob gets back in his car and decides it is time to go home. It is already late, and the sun has almost disappeared from the sky. Bob is almost home when he sees the town's gambling pub's bright new sign which helps to stimulate Bob's brain and distract from potentially, the worse day of his life. Steve then takes over.

Steve drives the car into the pub carpark. Many locals see Bob and gossip begins. Steve is unaware of this and heads towards the card table. Steve withdraws two hundred dollars and bets it at the card table. Steve has a great night and walks out with a total of four hundred dollars. He then buys some alcohol, from the liquor store, buys some drugs from the guy around the corner then drives to Bob's house. Steve goes inside and spends several hours consuming the drugs and alcohol. Bob eventually gets control back, long enough to see he has finished several bottles of spirits, a bag of white powder and a bag of green leaves. He then passes out.

Bob sleeps for two days straight. When he does wake, his bed stinks of urine, stale animal blood and alcohol. Bob has a vague memory of events. He gets up, speaks with his fish Leo Dafishy, puts his washing in the machine and has an exceptionally long shower.

Once he finishes in the shower, Bob goes to his fridge to see he has several bottles of soft drink in the fridge. He finishes one bottle of cola and begins the next. Full, he leaves the second bottle on the bench and goes for another lie down, accidentally falling asleep. When he wakes, he is hungry and goes looking for food. He has now not eaten for two and a half days. On his way to the cupboard, he sees his half-finished bottle of cola. The lack of food allows Bob's brain to become more easily distracted and triggered by boredom. This leads to Zion taking over.

Instead of Bob eating food, Zion begins performing experiments with the cola. At first these are harmless experiments leaving food and drink mess all over Bob's kitchen. However, the experiments quickly turn less harmless as Zion begins mixing cleaning fluids with flammable fluids and with various food items. Eventually, Zion accidentally causes a chemical fire. This leads to a poisonous gas to begin rising. It triggers the apartment's fire alarms leading to everyone in the complex being woken.

The fire brigade is called by one of Bob's neighbours. They arrive just as Bob regains control. Bob attempts to explain what has happened but he is ignored. The fire fighters put out the chemical fire and tell Bob they will be speaking with the police to press charges for wilful property damage. They then leave Bob's residence. As Bob begins closing his door, he sees many of the other residents shaking their heads at him.

Bob finds the final bottle of spirits that Steve had bought and drinks it clean then falls asleep.

The events of the last few months have caused rumours and gossip to swirl and escalate in Lackyer Vale. The events of the last three days had only intensified this gossip. His parents hear about the events and are worried. They attempt to call Bob on multiple occasions, but he does not answer.

Bob had chosen to turn his phone off so no one could call him, especially not the police. He knew that the fire department was going to be charging him for starting a chemical fire. He did not know his parents had been trying to call him. He also did not know that his work foreman had attended the police station and pressed charges, his female former colleagues had gone to the police station and pressed sexual harassment charges, and that the salesperson had also put in a report of attempted theft. When Bob eventually wakes it is nighttime.

Bob is unsure what day it is now, but he knows he needs food. He gets into his car and decides to drive to the nearest pizza drive thru. On his way to the pizza place, Bob sees a sign about crosswords. This sign, combined with the lack of proper food for at least the last three days, combined with the multitude of stressors, leads to Jessie taking over. Jessie continues driving and misses the turn off for the pizza place. Instead, Jessie is focused on crossword puzzles and then runs a red light.

Unfortunately, a police officer was at the lights going the opposite direction when Jessie ran the light. The officer attempts to have Bob pull over. Instead, Jessie who is oblivious to all that has transpired, continues driving until they accidentally drive into a stop sign. The police officer runs towards Bob's vehicle. The officer asks Bob for his name. Bob begins to regain control and is confused. The officer then asks again for Bob's name, and Bob begins slurring his world. The officer then tells Bob he is under arrest and attempts to handcuff him. Neon takes over and starts being sarcastic to the officer. Then Clarence takes over and yells at the officer. Then Laura takes over and excuses themselves. The officer is confused. The police officer's confusion regarding the behaviours they are witnessing, lead to them deciding to taser Bob.

Bob wakes in the nearby town in their mental health hospital. The officer's report, combined with the various reports from the Lackyer Vale locals, combined with the parents' own concerned report at the police station, led the emergency doctor to assume mental illness.

When Bob wakes, he is questioned by the psychiatrist. Bob has a vague idea based on his third person perspective of events but does not have the language to explain them well. Eventually after several hours of conversations with hospital's mental health social worker, combined with the screening results, the psychiatrist deduces that Bob is experiencing D.I.D.

Legally, Bob is lucky, most of the charges had insufficient evidence. Regarding the work charge, there was video evidence that Bob was provoked by the foreman. Regarding the theft attempt, no products were actually stolen, and the video evidence showed that Bob was dropping them as he was leaving the store. Regarding the sexual harassment charge, there was insufficient evidence and some people who were at the bakery shared that Bob was the one who had been attacked. However, Bob was charged with reckless driving.

After several more hours with the mental health nurse and the psychiatrist, it was confirmed that Bob had developed D.I.D. With assistance from Bob's parents, it was confirmed that Bob had a stressful childhood. It was also confirmed that Bob's very odd behaviours began after he was hit in the head by an unknown object.

Bob agrees to seek treatment and is able to stay in the town's mental health hospital for twelve months. After twelve months of treatment by Bob's mental health team that includes his psychologist, psychiatrist, occupational therapist and disability support team, Bob has recovered to a new "good enough" level of functioning. He now has a great team around him with three very passionate support workers who now live with Bob on a rotating roster.

They help Bob with his daily functioning, ensure Bob takes his medication and help to look after Leo Dafishy.

Bob's psychologist works with Bob weekly via telehealth and his psychiatrist works with Bob on a monthly basis via telehealth.

Eventually, Bob is able to return to working at the meat abattoir at a reduced capacity. Bob continues working at the abattoir until he retires at age seventy.

Bob's new mental health and support team are an example of how well sharing of information, working as a team, and treating the client as a person can lead to positive outcomes, helping not just the person but also society by allowing the person to contribute back to society in their own way.

The End.

Alternate Ending 2? – Coma?

Bob finally awakes from a coma. His eyes attempt to focus. He blinks at a rapid rate. His eyes struggle to focus as they have not been used for a long time. Bob's room is dimly lit with a neon light at the back of the room. Bob's fingers and toes begin twitching. Bob's body feels odd, almost foreign. He is unsure why, but he is shocked that his skin is not green. He is also unsure why he is disappointed that he cannot float.

Bob has been in hospital for fifteen years. Fifteen years ago, while Bob was walking to his car, something hit him in the head (as evidenced by a scar), and on his way down to the ground he hit his face on the car. Bob was found by a meat abattoir colleague who called the ambulance. Bob's parents found his pet in the apartment and felt that it was important to Bob, so they looked after it until it died.

During the fifteen-year coma, Bob's parents Jessica and Jason had been visiting his bed side, at first daily, then weekly, then eventually once a month. Both Doctor Clarence and Doctor Neo had been the main care providers with the many nurses including the head nurse Zion and registered nurses Ron, Steve and Laura also providing support over the last fifteen years.

Bob's vision is beginning to improve. He hears his parents' voices from the door and turns his head. At first Bob does not recognise his parents, they look very old compared to the last time he saw them. He attempts to say something but has forgotten how to speak, even though he still understands language.

The doctors congratulate Bob for waking and then leave Zion to explain everything. Zion explains how Bob had been found unconscious by a colleague at the meat abattoir. Bob then listens as

Zion and his parents explain what has been happening while Bob was in a coma. Bob is saddened to hear that Leo Dafishy had died.

Bob then spends the next two years regaining his strength and seems to have an internal drive that he had never shown or experienced before. It appears his imagination over the last fifteen years might have had some positive changes. With the support of the hospital's physiotherapists and occupational therapists, Bob is up and walking in no time.

With this second chance in life Bob starts going to a public gym for the first time in his life. He quits his job at the meat abattoirs and begins writing fiction novels. He finds it easiest to write in the mornings, with his dreams filling the pages. Within a six-month period, Bob has written many fiction novels about aliens, the power of death, universal battles and rebirth.

Twelve months after finding a publisher for his books, he sells his one hundred thousandth copy. Bob celebrates by taking his parents out to the local pub.

The next day Bob goes to hospital for his final check-up. He is sitting in the waiting room thinking about his book sales and how fortunate the fifteen-year coma was for him. As a joke to himself he finds the oldest person in the waiting room and clicks his fingers.

The elderly gentleman falls to the ground. Dead?

The End.